Uncle and the Hiccups

Written by Jill Eggleton
Illustrated by Brent Chambers

Uncle Ted was staying
with the twins.
They liked him.
He made everyone laugh.
He made faces and
he played tricks.

2

But when he stayed,
they always had pasta.
The twins didn't like pasta.
"It looks like slugs," they said.
And they gave their pasta
to the dog.

One night,
they had spaghetti.
The twins didn't even
like spaghetti.

"It looks like worms,"
they said.
"We don't like
to eat worms.
Worms are yucky!"

Uncle Ted loved it.
But he ate
the spaghetti so fast,
he got the hiccups.

SNiFF
SNiFF

5

The hiccups
went on and on.
The twins gave Uncle Ted
a big glass of water,
but the hiccups didn't stop.

"I think I'll go upside
down," said Uncle Ted.

Uncle Ted went upside down,
but the hiccups didn't stop.

"I'll have to go
to the doctor," he said.

When Uncle Ted
went to get his keys,
the twins got
their wolf masks.
They hid in the bushes.

Uncle Ted came
down the steps.
The twins jumped out and
went . . . *rraaa!*

But when the twins came in,
Uncle Ted was laughing.
"I'm not going
to the doctor," he said.
"I don't have the hiccups
any more."

The twins sat down
at the table again.
The spaghetti was still
on their plates.

Uncle Ted looked
at the twins.
"You can't have
cold worms,"
he said.
"We'll go out
for pizza."

At the pizza place,
the twins had pizza.
A man gave them some masks.

"Good," said the twins.
"We can scare you again
if your hiccups come back!"

Instructions
How to Make a Mask

You need:

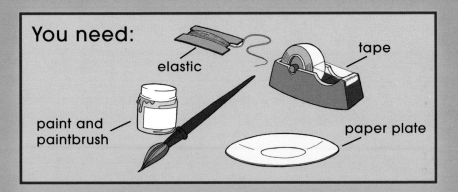

elastic

tape

paint and paintbrush

paper plate

Make the mask:

1.

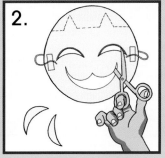

2.

1. Put the elastic on the plate with the tape.

2. Cut out the eyes and the mouth.

3.

3. Paint the mask.

Guide Notes

Title: **Uncle Ted and the Hiccups**
Stage: Early (4) – Green

Genre: Fiction
Approach: Guided Reading
Processes: Thinking Critically, Exploring Language, Processing Information
Written and Visual Focus: Instructions
Word Count: 267

THINKING CRITICALLY
(sample questions)
- What do you think this story could be about? Look at the title and discuss.
- Look at the cover. Why do you think Uncle Ted has his hand over his mouth?
- Look at pages 2 and 3. What other food do you think could look like slugs?
- Look at pages 6 and 7. What else do you think Uncle Ted could do to get rid of his hiccups?
- Look at pages 8 and 9. How do you know that the masks scared Uncle Ted?
- Look at pages 10 and 11. Why do you think Uncle Ted's hiccups went away?
- Look at page 14. Why do you think the children were given masks at the pizza place?

EXPLORING LANGUAGE

Terminology
Title, cover, illustrations, author, illustrator

Vocabulary
Interest words: hiccups, pasta, twins, spaghetti, keys, upside down
High-frequency words: everyone, gave, even, always, think
Positional words: upside down, in, out, inside, on
Compound words: inside, everyone

Print Conventions
Capital letter for sentence beginnings and names (**U**ncle **T**ed), periods, commas, exclamation marks, quotation marks